Friends Learn About Tobin

Written and Illustrated
by Diane Murrell, LMSW

Designed by
Clara Thibeaux

FUTURE HORIZONS INC.

All marketing and publishing rights guaranteed to and reserved by

FUTURE HORIZONS INC.

721 W. Abram Street
Arlington, TX 76013

800.489.0727 Toll Free
817.277.0727
817.277.2270 Fax

www.FHautism.com
email: info@FHautism.com

Copyright ©2007. Diane Murrell. Story and illustrations.

Cataloging in Publication Data is available from the Library of Congress.

ISBN: 1-932565-41-8

ISBN 13: 978-1-932565-41-6

Dedicated to

Linda Friedberg, Dr. Max Mintz and Dr. David Wood,
for accepting, enjoying and believing in Tobin

Tobin is a wonderful red engine who is learning to make lots of friends. He lives at the station with all the other trains.

This is Tobin. On the outside, he looks just like all the other trains. But inside, because of the way Tobin was built, he sometimes acts a little differently. Some things are hard for Tobin, some things are easier. That's true for everyone.

In another book, not this one, Tobin learned that sometimes he had to make changes to play well with other trains and have friends. In this book, Tobin's friends learn how to understand Tobin and his differences. Friends help friends whether they are the same or not.

One of Tobin's friends is called Limon. He is a lemony-lime green engine. Limon was puzzled when he saw Tobin in the yard. Tobin had puffed and puffed so much smoke out of his smoke stack that a cloud was covering him. "What's up, Tobin?" Limon asked.

"I don't like the new train staring at me. If I stay under the smoke, he can't see me," replied Tobin.

"It's okay. I'll tell him you don't like to be stared at," Limon said.

Limon is a good friend because he helps the new engine understand that Tobin feels bothered if someone stares at him.

Tobin was going slowly down the track. "Hurry, hurry," said his driver. "We are going to be late for the next stop. FLY! Tobin, FLY! So we can make it on time."

BOUNCE, BOUNCE, BOUNCE, went Tobin's wheels. "What are you doing?" asked the driver.

"I'm trying to fly, but I can't get off the ground!" Tobin replied.
"Oh, my bad!" said the driver. "When I said *FLY!* I meant *go fast.* Go as fast as if you were flying."

Tobin expects words to mean EXACTLY what they say. Sometimes words can mean more than one thing. Fly can mean "fly in the air" or it can mean "go fast." Next time, the driver will think about his words before talking to Tobin.

It is Jason the big yellow engine's birthday. Jason and Tobin are very good friends. Tobin loves parties, but today he is in the tunnel.

"Why is Tobin in the tunnel?" a train asked. "Oh, the crowd is too noisy for his ears and too busy for his eyes," explained Jason. "After a while, Tobin goes into the tunnel to take a rest." Jason understands Tobin and is glad he came to the party, even if Tobin takes a break for some quiet time.

"Down the track, engine in front, little blue cart in the back. Clickety clack, clickety clack. Down the track." Sometimes Tobin likes the sound of words and he will say them or sing them over and over and over and over and over and over and over again.

clickety clack clickety clack clickety clack clickety clack clickety clack clickety

After 20 times… **"AAAAAAH STOP!"** said Jock the train, who was working with Tobin. But Tobin could not stop the words. "Down the track, engine in front, little blue cart in the back. Clickety clack, clickety clack. Down the track."

"Why won't he **STOP?**" cried Jock. "Let me explain," said the engine driver. "Sometimes, words get stuck in his head and we have to wait for them to get **u-n-s-t-u-c-k**. It's a little thing he can't change, just like you can't change how you have a deep sounding whistle."

"Phoop! Phoop!" Jock whistles while the other trains go, "Pheep! Pheep!"

Sarah the pink engine chugged by Tobin and Limon very slowly and sadly. "What are you doing?" Limon asked. "This is the third time in 30 minutes that you have chugged by us."

"Oh, Limon, I have a new route that no one knows and I am lost. I can't remember where to go."

"Ask Tobin," said Limon. "He has the best memory in the station. He only needs to see a route once and he remembers it forever."
Tobin was happy to help and told Sarah exactly where to go and put her on the right track.

One day as Tobin was going down the track he saw a small piece of metal that had torn away from the rail. **Screek!!** His wheels came to a halt. "I can't go over that!" he shrieked indignantly. The little piece of stuckout metal bothered his mind so much he would not budge.

The driver pushed and pushed, but Tobin would not budge. When something is out of place, it upsets his mind. Finally, the driver had to get a hammer and beat the metal back down on the track. Then Tobin went over it. Actually, everyone was glad Tobin had made a fuss because he got the track fixed for all the trains.

Tobin gets used to things being a certain way and does not like them to change. When things stay the same, he feels calm and happy. When things change, it makes him feel nervous or afraid.

As they travel the route to the big station there is a detour...

THIS WAY! pointed the arrow. "Slow down, Tobin, something is on the track!" shouted the driver.

Tobin remembered his old route and did not want to change that plan so he ignored the sign.

He went straight through the DETOUR sign and sent it flying into the air. *Oops!* He ran right into a tree that had fallen on the track. He hit the tree so hard he fell off the track.

"Ouch! That must have hurt," said Jason who came to help. "You have a hard time making changes don't you Tobin? You like things to stay the same."

"That's ok," said the driver. "We understand you couldn't get yourself to stop and change the route. Next time we'll try to let you know much earlier if there is a change so you can get ready."

"Thanks," Tobin smiled.

"Why is Tobin always back at the roundhouse first?" asked Tiny one day. "It's not fair that he always gets to come home first."

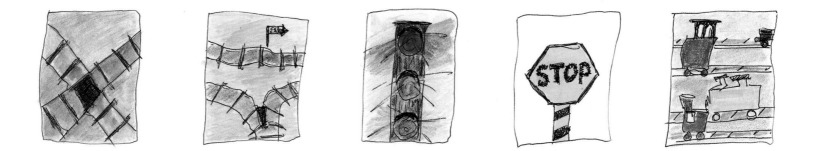

"Well," said the driver, "do you see Tobin's funnel at the back? It means he is a little different. All the messages Tobin gets — from his engine, from the tracks, from the driver — all take a long time to get sorted out in his mind so he knows where to go and how fast.

It is much more tiring for Tobin than for you to sort out these messages and then move down the track. He gets tired quicker than the other trains do. So we let him finish early to rest."

Tiny looked at the driver, "Maybe next time I can help Tobin by repeating some of the messages?" "That's a very good idea, Tiny!" smiled the driver.

"Come on, Big Fella!" shouted Nathan the orange train to Tobin.

"Don't call me *Big Fella*. My name is *Tobin*," said Tobin.

TOBIN

Tobin's driver explained to Nathan that Tobin gets upset if he thinks you have changed his name. Nathan was a kind train who didn't want his friend to be upset, so he shouted, "Come on, Tobin!"

"Hey! What are you doing, Rommel?" asked Tobin.

"I've got to fill my coal cars with coal and I don't know how many pieces will fill them up.

...66...79...83...94...101."

"I know! I know!" shouted Tobin. "It's three thousand one hundred and fifty-nine (3,159) pieces of coal."
"Wow! How do you know that Tobin?" asked the stationmaster. Tobin blushed. "I don't know, but I've always been able to do that."

The other trains had seen Tobin's special ability too and said, "That's right! Tobin always knows exactly how many pieces of coal fit into a coal car without counting."

It was a beautiful day in early winter. There were no leaves left on the trees. The driver and Tobin were going to visit the driver's friend.

Down the tracks and through the woods. "Oh no," cried Tobin. "I hate this! I hate when little twigs and leaves brush against me. They hurt and make me feel bad."

"I know," said the driver. "I have a cousin like you, Tobin. He hates scratchy clothes or labels to touch him. He gets all fidgety and acts prickly when he feels light touch. We will find a different way home for you."

Tobin has some wonderful friends. They like him with his differences. When Tobin acts differently to them, they ask him if something is bothering him or if he needs their help. Sometimes Tobin feels overwhelmed by too many things going on at once. Then the trains help Tobin feel comfortable and safe.

Tobin loves his engine friends. He accepts their differences too. Together, they all find things that are the same about each other and things that are different.

Pheep Pheep! Phoop Phoop! Phee Phee! Peep Peep! Pip Pip! Pheep Pheep!!

"We are ALL trains!" the engines whistled.

Originally from Northern Ireland, Diane Murrell works, plays, and does research as a social worker in Houston, Texas. She has four indomitable sons who tease her mercilessly, one of whom inspired this book. Diane has a heart for mothers and children to find their place in the community, and will tame monsters and slay dragons to help this happen through her life and work. In addition to the Tobin series, she is author of *Oliver Onion*, a children's book and study guide about self-acceptance.